The Magical Gray Flower:
The Power of Self-Love

By Alexandra Angheluta

Illustrated by Romina Petra

Printed in the United States of America
First Printing, 2018
ISBN 9781534987326
Library of Congress Control Number:
2017964561
www.PlaySittersHawaii.com

You may not believe it, but I was once a seed
In the dark soil I was no larger than a bead

I felt very alone and scared in the dirt
For I was small, frail and on the alert

There were worms, beetles, and fire ants all around me
I was scared that fresh air would never find me

I was planted in a spot where there was no light
The warmth from the sun never touched me just right

I waited day by day to feel a ray
All I could feel was cold, it was so gloomy and gray!

Somedays water would come
Other days I would receive none

With no flow for my soul, I was so thirsty and dry
I was lost in the darkness, this I cannot deny.

I didn't feel accepted and became quite neglected
All I wanted was to feel connected.

I saw fancy flowers above the compost
I knew this too is what I wanted most

The roses – Oh what a treat to smell so sweet.

The lilies so innocent and pure
I was convinced they felt no fear.

The tulips stood so tall and strong
All I wanted was to just belong!

I wanted to be like them so I gave it a try,
I jumped and sprouted straight towards the sky!

Oh my! What a dismay!
I had no color, I was just plain gray

Being this color gave me a big frown
I was left feeling like I was a letdown

My leaves kept falling and my petals were dull
My scent simply would not attract a soul.

Even the bees flew right by me,
They just wouldn't try me.

After a while I had no joy to give
Though flowers should spread happiness as long as they live.

This made me feel horrible
It really was unbearable.

I felt like I had nothing to offer the world being gray.
Every day I was filled with dismay

Then I realized this is unacceptable,
A flower to not have color is just unimaginable

I pressed my leaves together and prayed for light
I asked for an endless supply of water, I was very polite!

And then a voice responded, she sounded like a genius
She said that I hold the key to a secret ingredient

The voice said that within me I hold the power,
That I can imagine myself as any sort of flower

That my own lack of love is the reason that I didn't glow
The voice assured me:

"Accept yourself and surely you will be as bright as a rainbow"

So I imagined my journey and stuck to my plan
I chose to become my biggest fan

I loved each petal
Even though they were the color of metal

I changed my thoughts
I embraced my faults.

It didn't matter that my soil was dark,
I was now ready to ignite my spark.

I spoke to myself very quietly at first, I whispered

"I love myself for all that I am"

As the days went on I repeated my mantra:

"I love myself! I love myself! I love myself!!"

I began to believe it with all of my roots
I shouted louder, it was kind of a hoot

"I love myself! I love myself! I love myself!!"

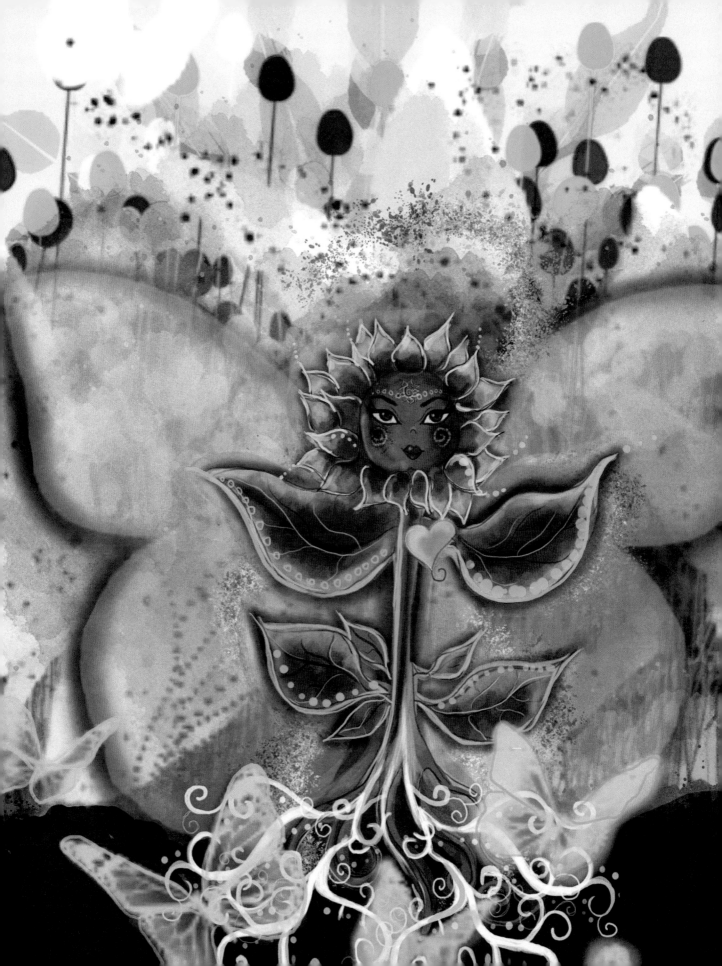

You wouldn't believe what happened next
I must admit I felt very perplexed

It was so magical how radiant I became
My heart felt as if it was reclaimed

I trusted in myself, I didn't quit
Now I feel like I am truly sunlit

I'm in a place where nothing could harm me
I feel safe, I feel peace
I feel completely at ease

Guess who even comes by to visit me?

The bees!

I spread happiness all around me,
The garden gates are open, come join me

Choose to plant yourself where you desire,
And you will see that you have never felt higher

You are unique, You are exceptional
Your perfection is really quite a spectacle

You are the ONLY ONE in this garden of life.

Here are the steps to be the best you can be:

Believe you are in fact love.
Receive nothing but love.
Give Love.

It's all you need to feel as peaceful as a dove.

Dear Readers,

   This story is my memoir. As a child and young adult I went through experiences that caused me to feel a lot of sadness. Only through self-awareness, self-care and self-love did I find my happiness. The flower in the story symbolizes my own personal transformation.

Thank you to all the children who helped me bloom.

Advice from a Sunflower:

" Be bright, sunny and positive. Spread seeds of happiness, rise, shine and hold your head high "

About the Author

Alexandra C. Angheluta MSW, LSW is a Hawaii Licensed Social Worker and the owner of PlaySitters Hawaii: Using the Educational and Therapeutical Value of Play. She was born in a small town in Romania and immigrated to America as a young child. Using the Law of Attraction, she planted herself in Hawaii as a young adult and created a life that allowed her to spend her time with children in the magical world of play. She believes in truth, freedom and love.

About the Illustrator

Romina Petra has been creating masterpieces on walls since she was a young child in Romania. As she grew, she was able to gain an educational background which consisted of graphic design and digital art. This led her to discover her innate passion: providing an artistic fantasy world for children. Being able to experiment with her creativity through the use of shapes, colors and giving life to words is where Romina was able to find her own path in adding color to the world.

Made in the USA
Middletown, DE
16 December 2019